ISBN: 978-1-0690034-7-8

We Are A Thought,

Which Lingers,

On The Brink Of Finality,

And Stays Far Too Long.

A NOVEL BY
CRYSTAL ELIZABETH WESTMAN

Intoxicated Witch 2

TABLE OF CONTENTS

Epiph· any

[ɪˈpɪfəni]

Noun

- A manifestation of a divine or supernatural being: "many believe this scene to represent an epiphany of the goddess"

- A moment of sudden and great revelation or realization: "a few years ago, I had an epiphany" { from Oxford Languages}

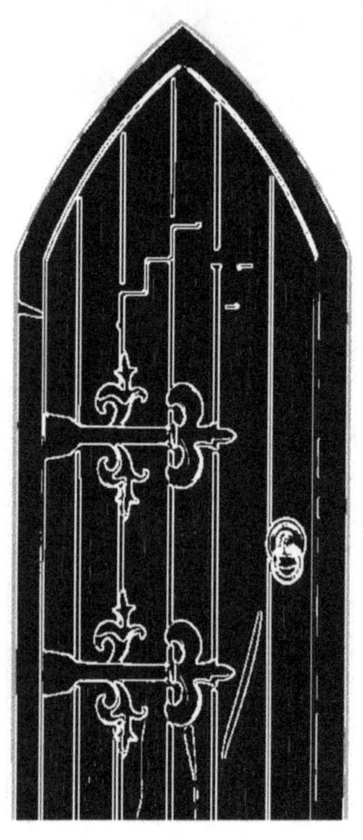

ENDING A

The meter reads: $11:00

The time: 11:11 am

The startling sound of honking can be heard from the other side of the globe. Drivers are enraged, people are shouting, and our driver is no exception, "hey, buddy, move your ass already!"

I am suddenly transported to a state of complete and total shock. Am I dreaming? What the hell's going on out there? I haven't had my coffee yet. The meter is paused. We're just imprisoned in a sea of traffic. With the crate squished between the two us, I look over to see Patrick poking his head out to investigate the hold up.

My mind is racing. In a mild state between stoned and completely fucked—I panic. I can't be here. I can't do this. How am I in a cab with Patrick anyway – why'd I get in?

My internal compass is pointing towards the door. One hand quickly reaches over and pulls the handle, and I dash out just in time.

Patrick doesn't have time to react. "Ha, ha!" I yell to the skies.

Then in a split second I'm gone—and can be seen running for my sanity all the way home to my bed.

"Ah, bed, how I love you so."

I lay awake a few moments, rolling over onto

the same bag of Cheetos from the day before, and feel surprisingly okay for a girl who just ran away from a man she thought she loved.

Then it hits me. I do love Patrick, but I also love myself. I somehow have the ability to feel multiple things all at the same time: love, hate, anger, pain, hunger. My stomach rumbles and I don't know what to do with myself.

Dammit, I'm starving. It's been hours since I've eaten anything substantial, but I can't seem to roll myself out of bed to make something. Where is a gourmet chef when you need one?

I gotta write that down, *hire Gordon Ramsay*

When suddenly there's a knock at my door.

"Uh oh, what'd I do now?" I worry, imagining a police officer getting ready to cuff me. I mean it's a perfectly reasonable fear, I tell myself, especially after the bender I just had—whew! Who knows what I got into last night.

That's when I hear, "Flora! Are you in there?"

I freeze.

It's Patrick of all people. What on earth is he doing here?

"Flora-a-a-a!"

Well, he's got quite the set of pipes on him. I

8

consider waiting it out, letting him scream until he loses his voice, but then on second thought, the neighbors will make a fuss if I let it go on for much longer.

So, I yell back, "who is it?"

Chuckling

"Oh, come on Flora, you know it's me, open up!"

"Me—who?" I shout.

"Flora, I just want to be sure you're okay. You ran out of the cab like a crazy person."

I stand vindictively at the door, "hmm, funny, so NOW you want to know if I'm alright."

"Um, well, yes, Flora, I imagine you are still coming down from whatever you took last night, and it's not good to be left alone. Can you just let me inside already."

I pause to think about it a few seconds more.

"Flora? I can't hear anything. What's happening?"

Curled up in a ball, I plop myself down on the other side of the door and proceed to carry on the conversation with Patrick.

"I'm here. I'm just thinking."

"Okay, good, that's good. What ya thinking about?"

"About you—me—us."

"I know."

"Oh, you think you know, Patrick, but you don't have a clue as to what I'm thinking."

"Go on, enlighten me, then."

*Patrick's back is slouched against the other side of the door, head against the wall, he and Flora find themselves with nothing more than a door between them. *

"Well, first of all, it is not okay how you just left me like that. You just abandoned me without an explanation. One day you were here, the next day you were gone."

Patrick wasn't used to Flora being so

emotionally direct with him. She would usually just cuss him out or pout like a child in the corner. He was pleasantly surprised to be having a real conversation for once...

"I know, I was wrong how I left, and I'm very, truly, sorry. I really am, but I just didn't know what else to do."

"You could have stayed and tried to work things out. That's what you do, Patrick, that is what you do when you have a fight!"

"I know, I just honestly didn't know how."

"No, you mean you didn't want to. Probably because you were cursed!"

My voice raises and my blood starts to boil.

"Cursed?

"Yes, that woman you've been hanging around put a curse on you, and I know it."

"Ha, pfft, okay, Flora, now we're heading into the deep end. Nobody has placed any curses or has done any creepy hocus pocus on anyone. I left of my own volition, I left because I needed to, and that's that."

I take a moment to inhale the words he just said.

It took only a few seconds more for me to realize I had been wasting my breathe on a man who was never going to change. He would never be who I needed him to be. He was never going to be the person who stays when times get tough, or the person who came home an hour later after a fight to say sorry. "Well, in that case, Patrick, I am done. I can't do this anymore. If you could so easily

13

just run away and choose yourself... this time I'm choosing myself. I love you, but I need so much more than this. I need stability, and someone who fights for us when things get tough, not someone who just gives up."

"Wait, Flora, I'm here now aren't I?" he reasons.

I pause to reconsider and then change my mind.

"Patrick, it's too little, too late, there's nothing more you can say or do. We both need help. I need to do what's best for me now."

Things weren't going the way he had hoped.

He thought if he came to see Flora, that

maybe they could find some common ground. But here they are in the midst of entropy.

Waiting for the universe to close in on itself, he just knows, deep down, nothing will ever be the same again.

ENDING B

The meter reads: $11:00

The time: 11:11 am

Patrick holds me tightly as we pull up to my driveway. The taxi pulls in and Patrick gives me a look like, 'shall I come in?'

He walks me to my doorstep and holds me still. Within seconds we begin making out and he whisks me away to my beloved bed, *"oh, bed, how I've missed you."*

I then roll over and whisper to Patrick, "how I've missed you, too."

We pull the covers over us and hold each other close, relieved to finally be home.

ENDING C

The meter reads: $11:00

The time: 11:11 am

The taxi is zig zagging though traffic. Patrick is saying something mid-sentence out the window. I hear chirping and sirens and smell the morning, when an abrupt halt flies me directly into the abyss. Silence sneaks up without warning. I hear the car alarm going off. Now a group of people are crowding around. One says, "It looks bad, call an ambulance!"

CHAPTER ONE

FLORA WAKES UP

Footsteps echo eerily down the sterile, dimly lit corridor. The faint scent of antiseptic clings to the air, mingling with the distant hum of medical equipment. my heart pounding with a desperate urgency as I glance over my shoulder, certain that someone is watching. They're always watching.

Choose a door, any door, which one's it gonna be, where's it gonna lead!

DOOR 1: I kick it open with a *"huh-take that!"* then continue hobbling towards the finish line, down the winding hallway towards wherever it is I'm going, I can't seem to remember. I look down and it appears I've been injured, but I can't recall how.

I then turn the corner where I am instantly transported to the backseat of a swerving vehicle.

Out of the corner of my peripheral, our taxi driver is holding the steering wheel down with his head. I can't see Patrick. Someone's now lifting me up into a vehicle. Am I being abducted?

"Sneaky aliens..."

Moments later — *I wake up.*

I'm in an unidentifiable room.

Where am I?

Whose bed is this?

HOSPITAL FROM HELL

I look around to catch my bearings. My eyes are adjusting to the flickering lights, the smell of bleach smells strong enough to kill me, but I presume it's because cleanliness is next to godliness, as they say. All I know is it's giving me a headache.

They've got me hooked up to a machine that won't stop beeping, "someone help! I'm trapped on planet earth and they're holding me against my will."

A young woman in a pink hospital uniform emerges, and says a few words to another taller, and much older woman in a white jacket that turns to fetch a gurney.

The nurse enters my room with an alarmingly chirpy demeanor, "good morning sleepy head!" she says, grinning ear to ear like a porcelain doll with a painted smile.

How am I supposed to respond to that? I wonder. I'm in the hospital goddammit and have no idea how I got here. Rather than shoving some happy go lucky crap down my throat, why don't you tell me what's going on!

But instead of saying that, I take the high road and muster up some energy to respond with a reasonable tone— "excuse me, Miss. Nurse, can you please tell me why I'm here?"

She shoots me a look of sympathy before giving me the go-around, "oh, I wish I could, but I'm not at liberty to say sweetheart. The doctor shall be in shortly and she'll explain everything."

"But I'd just really like to get going... you know. I'm fine, really. Please just have the doctor sign off for me and I'll be out in a jiffy," I explain, gasping for air.

The nurse is now looking quite concerned. I can see this conversation is quickly spiraling out of control and there's nothing I can do. They've clearly got me where they want me— in some sort of hostage situation. Or quite possibly these phonies are actually aliens masquerading as human beings – wearing meatsuits we call bodies, disguised as doctors – that's got to be what's going on, there's no other explanation.

She tries to let me down easy, "well, I'm afraid I just can't do that, Miss. Blume. Please eat your meal and the doctor will be in to see you shortly."

She wheels the food cart back out into the hall. Behind her is the receptionist's desk with your usual suspects: a receptionist is taking calls, a man stands beside her holding a document, while a visitor stands on the other side waiting for her to get off the phone. Directly behind the receptionist is a metal bookshelf, and on that shelf sits a perfectly placed milkcrate.

I can't explain why exactly – but I recall

Patrick in the back seat of a taxi. My head's spinning so fast I can barely make out the rest.

"Where is Patrick?" I wonder. I imagine he probably took off and left me here alone to fend for myself.

"Just great..."

Forget him, he's on his own. It's each one for himself now, no more chances. Leave me once, I forgive ya, leave me twice, I scorn ya.

While mulling over the idea of him escaping from the hospital without me, I'm quickly distracted by the thought of these thieves trying to steal my stuff. Who do they think they are—holding me here like a prisoner. I demand answers, dammit.

I have no other option than to devise a plan to get out of here. "Good thing all our tax dollars go to this," I tell myself, while slowly trying to catch my balance.

No one tells you how hard it is to walk after an accident.

I pause

There's a clear delay while my mind tries to piece things together, "that's right—there was an accident."

The memories come flashing back out of sequence: *taxi, bed, Patrick, ambulance, beach, bar, hospital room* – blank, blank,

blank.

I'm now two steps away from the door when the doctor appears in front of me. She has disheveled black hair and looks like she's been up all night partying, though, I'm aware that's probably just my default setting, she's clearly been working the night shift.

"So, Miss. Blume, how are we feeling today?" I look around the room confused to see no one other than myself, "WE are feeling like I was hit by a bus," I say facetiously.

"Oh, good, looks like your memory is coming back."

"Wait, what?" I ask. "I was hit by a bus?" I'm dumbfounded. Could that be true? At this point anything's possible.

"Sounds about right," she says, then proceeds to put on plastic gloves and a surgical mask. It feels like an episode of Greys Anatomy – only I'm the main character being left to figure out the ending to this nail-biting cliff hanger.

She assures me, "we can chat more about that later, "but what I need you to do now for me, Flora, is roll slightly over on your side so I can check your breathing."

Rolling over on my side

I'm totally, utterly, flabbergasted. What is going on? Trying to recall what happened the night before, I'm left with nothing but a void—I'm blanking out.

"Were you being serious just now? I'm pretty sure I'd remember being hit by a bus, I don't think that's what happened."

Doctor O'Hara smiles like she just told the world's funniest joke, "ah, you got me! You weren't really hit by a bus, but you may as well have been," she tells me, like that's a perfectly professional response.

I honestly don't know what to say.

She ignores my snide comments under my breath as she continues to examine me head to toe. "All set, Flora," she says. "You're just a little banged up. You've got a minor concussion, but it's nothing a little rest and recuperation can't fix. I'll be back to check on you later."

She gives me a pat on the back and then explains a psychiatrist would be conducting a standard psych evaluation next, which means more people I do not know hovering around me, withholding information.

Hmm, my ears perk up. Something about this place just doesn't feel right. Why on earth would they need to give me a psych test? There's nothing wrong with me.

It looks to be anywhere around eight to ten-o-clock at night. The streetlights are blinding, the road looks bare. I can't see why they wouldn't want to do this in the morning. I just hope whatever the reason is, it'll get me closer to being released from this gawd forsaken hell.

THE PSYCH EVALUATION

A nurse wheels me into a dark and dank office plastered with green wallpaper, and for no apparent reason, everything seems to have geese on it: the upholstery, the book ends, the curtains, heck, even the wooden duck sitting on the desk was staring me down.

Before I can even dare pop-a-wheelie with this wheelchair I don't really need to be using, The Doc comes barreling through the doors, slams his notebook down onto the desk with such disdain you'd think he needs psychological help.

"Flora Blume, the name's Dr. Powell, nice to

meet you. It seems you've had quite the night I see," he declares like he's met me before.

"I guess you could say that."

"Why don't you tell me about it," he prompts, quizzing me for the exam of a lifetime.

"That's the thing, Doc, I can't remember. Sorry but it's honestly all a blur."

"Yes, he says, that happens with minor head injuries, it's to be expected. "

He looks down at his notes and begins to read, "it says here you took a large quantity of hallucinogens, mixed with an inconceivable amount of alcohol, before being sent to the emerge to get your stomach pumped. You mean to say you don't recall a single thing from last night, not even a little?"

Discouraged, I try again. I'm scouring the halls of my memory searching for answers, but I've got nothing. I shrug as to say, 'I don't know, man, can you help me out, it feels like you know more than me. Tell me why we're here - what the meaning to life is - and where we all go when we disappear.'

He scribbles something into his notebook, hums and haws a bit before walking over to where a nurse places a milkcrate perfectly outside of his office, at his request. He puts it down onto the desk and looks in my direction, "how about this—can you tell me what this is?'

"A milkcrate?" I respond as if it were a trick.

It wasn't.

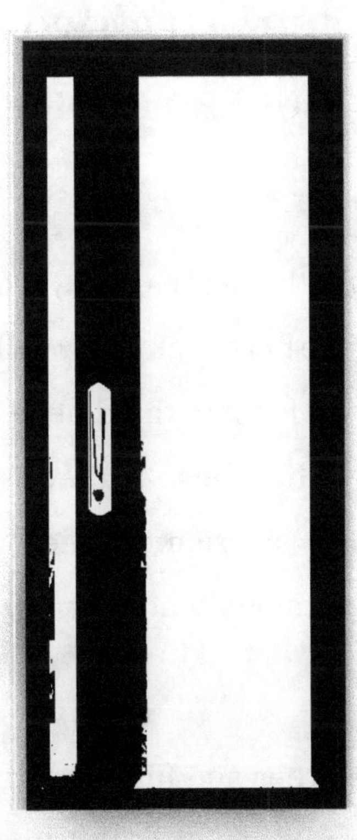

CHAPTER TWO
LOCKED DOORS

The doctors, the nurses—they were all in on it, keeping me here against my will. They said it's for my own good, that I need to recover. Confined within these whitewashed walls, drugged and disoriented, the only thing I know for certain is that I need to find a way out, and fast.

I turn the corner and find myself in another identical hallway, the fluorescent lights flickering ominously above. My breath quickened. How many hallways have I already wandered down? It felt like I'd been walking for hours, but every turn only led me deeper into the labyrinth. Panic clawed at my insides. There had to be an escape out of this maze. There had to be.

I pass a series of doors, each one identical to the last, (muttering to myself), "great, just great. They're all locked. How did I end up here, anyway?" Okay, Flora, focus. One of these doors has to lead out of this hospital.

Right then, as I was in the midst of feeling sorry for myself, at the end of the hall, there it was, slightly out of place in a modern hospital—its surface worn, as if it had been there for centuries. My pulse quickened—as its structure called out to me, whispering promises of freedom.

DOOR 2: A BRIGHT REFUGE

Without a second thought, I reach out and turn the handle. The door creaks open, and a rush of cool air hits my face. I step through and find myself standing in a small, dimly lit room. It was familiar, but I couldn't quite place it. The scent of pine and cold autumn air drifted in from a cracked window.

And then I saw him—Patrick, standing by the window, his back to me. He is dressed in the clothes he'd worn that night, the night of our fight. The night before he left.

"Patrick?" I whisper, my voice trembling.

He turns to face me, his expression unreadable. "Flora, what are you doing here?"

My heart ached at the sight of him. I remember now, the argument that had torn us apart, the harsh words that had echoed in this very apartment. It had been a few days shy of Halloween. He walked out and never came back.

"I came to find you," I told him, my voice breaking. "I need to get out of here, Patrick. They're keeping me in this hospital, but I don't belong here. I need to be with you."

Patrick shakes his head, his eyes full of sorrow. "Flora, you have to listen to me. You need to stay here. They're trying to help you."

"No," I insist, my hands trembling. "You don't understand. They're lying to me. They're trying to keep me locked up."

Patrick steps closer, his voice gentle but firm. "Flora, please. You were in an accident. You need to heal. The doctors, they're not your enemies. They're trying to save you."

I shake my head, tears streaming down my face. "No, Patrick, I need to be with you. We can make this right. We can fix what happened."

But Patrick's expression doesn't change. "You have to let go, Flora. It's time."

A wave of confusion and despair wash over me. The room begins to blur around the edges, and Patrick's figure wavers like a mirage. I reach out to him, but my hand passes through empty air. The room was dissolving, the door reappearing in front of me, leading me back to the hospital hallway.

"No!" I cried, my voice echoing in the void. "Patrick don't leave me! Please don't go!"

But it was too late. The door swings open, pulling me back through, and I find myself once again in the cold, sterile hallway of the hospital. I stumble, my knees buckling beneath me as I collapse to the floor, my sobs echoing throughout the building.

A soft hand touches my shoulder, and I look up to see a nurse kneeling beside me, concern etched on her face. "Flora, it's okay. You're safe. Let's get you back to your room."

My mind a tangled mess, I don't resist as the nurse helps me to my feet, guiding me gently back to my bed.

The hallway stretches endlessly before me, and I feel myself sinking into the ocean of despair.

As the nurse leads me away, I glance over my shoulder, half-expecting to see the door again, or perhaps Patrick standing at the end of the hall waiting. But there was nothing. Just the cold, impersonal walls of the hospital, closing in around me.

CHAPTER THREE
PSYCH WARD & A DAYDREAM

They tell me it's my second day here. Sitting in Doctor Powell's office, I stare out the window, my mind racing "Dr. Powell, there's something I need to ask you about."

Doctor Powell, (entering the room), "of course, Flora. What's on your mind?"

Turning to him, my face showing confusion, I keep thinking about Patrick. I feel so abandoned, he just left me here and walked away.

Doctor Powell is sitting down, doing his best to console me. "It's understandable to feel that way when you're in such a vulnerable state. Sometimes our memories can be distorted by emotion."

Sighing

"But what if it wasn't just a feeling? What if he really did leave me and he's never coming back?"

He carefully responds, "it's important to look at the situation from different angles. Your memories might not be telling the full picture at this time."

I'm becoming deeply frustrated, because I clearly remember waking up alone in this hospital. He must have abandoned me, of course he did.

He tries to go easy, "sometimes the mind can play tricks on us during traumatic events. It's possible that your perception of what happened was influenced by the stress and confusion of the accident--add in the consumption of narcotics, and you're bound to be confused.

My eyes welling up, I don't know if I can handle the thought of him leaving me again, when I was so scared and hurt the first time. It feels like such a betrayal.

Doctor Powell, sympathetically, "it's natural to feel that way. It's part of processing the events. However, there are aspects of the situation that might not be fully clear for you yet.

Desperately, I'm waiting for him to fade away into the background so I can make a run for it.

He says, "it's okay to take your time to process everything. The truth will become clearer as you continue to heal, and your memory comes back.

"I hope so. I just want to understand what really happened."

He reassures me, "you're making progress, Flora, It's a difficult journey, but you're not alone. We're here to help you through this.

I KNOW he's lying. There's something he's not telling me. I've been around liars my whole life: drunks, addicts, criminals, the scientifically inclined. I take a deep breath and exhale. "Thank you, Doctor, I'll try to be patient and keep working on it.

He stands up, "an excellent approach, remember, we're here to support you, in taking all the steps necessary to accelerate your healing."

Healing my ass. What does a doctor know that a witch doesn't.

That's right, I almost forgot—I am a witch.

I ponder ways to conjure up something while being a mouse inside this trap they call a healing facility. If only I knew where to get some fresh herbs. There has to be something lying around here somewhere. And with that, the start of a plan begins to unfold—sneak into he kitchen and the medicine cabinet—but as fast as I come up with a plan, I walk out of Doctor Powells office and forget.

THE UNFOLDING

Back in my room. I recall I've always had a knack for getting myself into odd situations. But this—this feels different. The room is eerily quiet, the only sound my heart thumping in my chest. I glance around, taking in the IV drip and the way the curtains flutter slightly as if a breeze were flowing through them, though I know there's no window.

I try to remember again how I got here. A lady dropped me off. No, that doesn't feel right. I close my eyes, straining to recall the details. Flashes come back—faces, sounds, chaos—but they slip away like sand through my fingers. The only thing that remains clear is a sense of dread, the overwhelming feeling that I shouldn't be here.

Panic rises within me. I swing my legs over the side of the bed, my bare feet touching the cool floor. I can't stay here. I pull the IV out, wincing at the sharp pain that follows. My head spins for a moment, but I shake it off. I need to escape.

I open the door cautiously, peering into the dimly lit corridor beyond. It's empty. I step out, my heart racing, the fluorescent lights flickering overhead like some kind of bad omen. The walls are sterile white, but I notice the peeling paint and scuffed floors, remnants of a place that has seen better days.

I make my way down the hallway, each step echoing in the silence. Rooms line both sides, doors slightly ajar. I pause outside one, straining to hear any sounds within.

A low murmur and voices drift out, and I catch snippets of words: *room eleven, eleven.*

What does that mean? I wonder.

I continue on, my instincts screaming at me to turn back, but curiosity propels me forward. I pass a window and glance outside. The sky is a bleak gray, casting a pall over everything. No signs of life. My heart sinks further.

Suddenly, I hear footsteps behind me. I whirl around, my breath hitching in my throat. A nurse appears, her expression unreadable. "You shouldn't be out of your room," she says, her voice calm yet firm.

"Why? What's happening?" I ask, my voice trembling.

"You're not ready," she replies, but I can't tell if she's speaking to me or to someone else entirely.

I take a step back, instincts kicking in. "I need to leave. Please, just let me go."

She shakes her head, a shadow of something dark crossing her face. "You can't. It's for your own good."

I bolt past her, my heart pounding, racing down the corridor. I can't let her stop me. I need to know what's going on. I duck into a nearby room, closing the door quietly behind me.

Inside, it's cluttered with old medical equipment and dusty files. I rummage through the drawers, hoping to find something—anything—that explains why I'm here. My fingers brush against a file labeled "Flora Blume," and I yank it out, flipping it open.

The words blur together as I read: "Patient suffering from severe dissociative amnesia.

Memory loss linked to trauma."

Panic surges again. Trauma? What trauma?

I slam the file shut, glancing nervously at the door. I can't let them find me. I take a deep breath, trying to calm my racing mind. There's got to be a way out.

Then I hear it—a distant noise, a beeping, coming from somewhere down the hall. It's rhythmic, almost like a heartbeat. I follow the sound, driven by a mixture of fear and desperation. Each step brings me closer to the truth, but also deeper into the unknown. As I approach a set of double doors, the beeping intensifies, and I know I have to push through. With a deep breath, I swing the door open, stepping into a bright, bustling area filled with doctors and nurses.

I take a moment to absorb the scene—people moving purposefully, machines whirring. But something feels off. No one acknowledges me. I glance around, anxiety gnawing at my insides, "HELP!" I cry out, but my voice is swallowed by the chaos.

That's when I realize: I'm invisible here. No one can see me. My heart races, a cold realization dawning. I'm not just trapped in a hospital. I'm trapped in my own mind, fighting to escape the shadows of a past I can't remember.

I take a step back, ready to retreat into the hallway, when a familiar face appears in front of me. It's someone I recognize from my fragmented memories.

"Flora," they say softly, a hint of recognition in their eyes. "You need to come with me."

And just like that, I'm pulled back into the unknown, teetering on the edge of memory and the abyss, trapped in this hell of my own making.

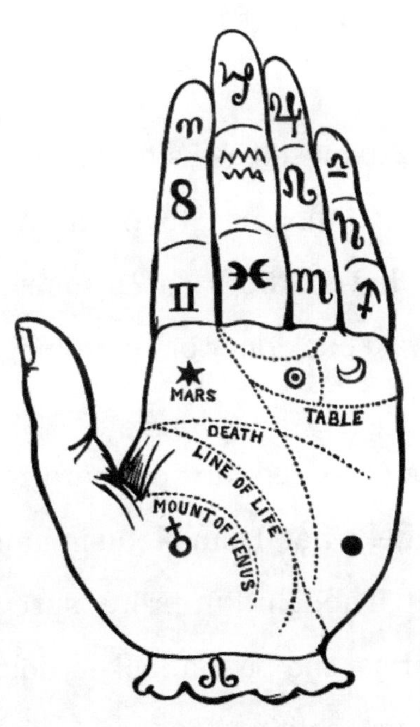

MARS
TABLE
DEATH
LINE OF LIFE
MOUNT OF VENUS

CHAPTER FOUR
ESCAPE ROUTE

Muttering to myself as I slip into the kitchen, okay, Flora, this has to be it. A kitchen. Kitchens have exits, right? I mean, they've gotta have a back door or something.

I try rifling through the cupboards. Maybe if I find a chef's hat, I can blend in and make a run for it. Though, I'm pretty sure a chef's hat won't get me past a locked door, hmm, what's a girl to do?

Now spotting a door— "There! That's got to be a way out." (I open the door and find a narrow staircase leading down) "Perfect!"

Descending the stairs, I'm finally getting out of here, and no one's gonna stop me! Suddenly I hear a loud beep and then a loud screeching over the intercom.

Wait, what's that?

I peek over the railing. Oh no. That sound— it's the fire alarm! Seriously, Flora? What did I trip over? I look down and see a puddle of water spreading.

Just great, a mop bucket of dirty floor water. Attempting to make a stealthy exit, I end up slipping and fall backwards instead. Okay, not so great. More like "it's all a wash."

Now, crawling on my knees, I awkwardly wade through the marsh of hospital fluids and god knows what else.

I'm just gonna—whoops! —try to stay low and quiet, I tell myself. If they find me now, I'll never live this down. I can't go to jail looking like a drenched lab rat.

A woman is now shouting, "the alarm's going off! We have to find whoever triggered it!"

I frantically try to disappear but cannot. The water's everywhere! I overhear dome kitchen staff say "we need to find the source! Who did this?"

A hospital admin barges though the doors and spots the trail of wet footprints. "Look!

Someone's tracks, it's clear someone around here set it off."

I try to hide behind a mop bucket, which isn't very effective, slinkying my way around the bucket, as if that would help. Maybe if I stay really still, they won't see me.

Walking directly over me, Is that you Flora? (trying to stay quiet), "Please don't see me. Please don't see me."

The admin peers around the room, we need to check under everything. Someone has to be crawling around here.

I sigh, defeated. So much for my great escape.

The nurse spots me behind the mop bucket. "There she is! Found her!"

I sit up, dripping wet. Well, this was fun. I didn't think my plan would involve an impromptu shower; I say aloud.

She helps me up. "Flora, you've set off the fire alarm and turned the kitchen into a water park. Not quite the escape you had in mind, huh?"

"Apparently, my escape skills need some work."

The doctor chimes in, "I think we need to add a new rule: no more unsupervised kitchen adventures. Got it?"

I give him a grin, "I promise, no more shenanigans."

The nurse is trying not to chuckle. "Let's get you dried off and back to your room before you cause any more mayhem."

Looking around the soaked kitchen, and back at the staff aiding my exit. "Well, at least I made a splash!"

The doctor (laughing), "that you did. Now let's get you back before you drown."

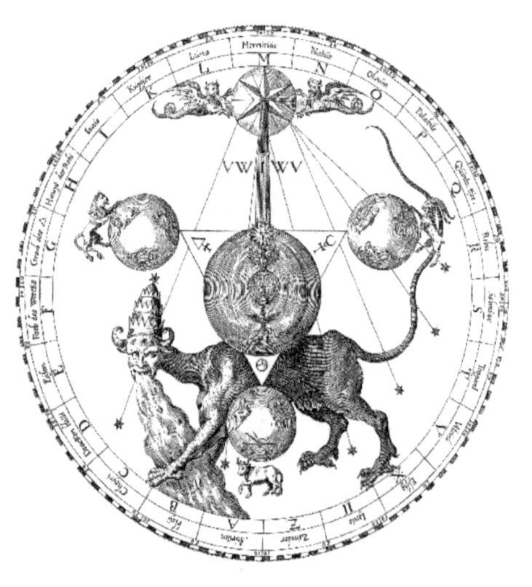

CHAPTER FIVE

TAKE ME WITH YOU

Now, lying in bed, I drift off into a trance where time meets infinity. I see a door and walk through.

DOOR 3: MEMORY LANE

Patrick is standing by the window. "Flora! You're here. I didn't think I'd see you again."

"Patrick! I thought you had left me here."

He's smiling, "no Flora, I've been waiting for you. I have something to show you.

Remember how we always talked about that trip we were gonna take, I finally made it happen."

Patrick pulls me closer, "I wanted to show you we can have everything we wanted, Flora. If you just stay here with me, we can stay here forever."

I hesitate, there's something not quite right.

Deep down I know it's all wrong.

"It's tempting, Patrick. But I really want out of this hospital."

Patrick sighs, "if you must, but remember, this is what we dreamed of. If you leave without me now, it might be gone forever.

I shake my head in disbelief—and then the nurse jostles me awake. "Time for dinner, Flora, tonight you'll have the chicken and mash served with a side of Jello."

"Yummy," I reply, my face clearly not aligning with my words.

"Just so you know dear, they tried to find an emergency contact for you, but we're having difficulty. Of course, with your memory not being one hundred percent and all. Would you know anyone we could call, your mom or dad perhaps?"

"My parents are dead." I retort.

She briefly pauses. "I see. You remember that much at least."

Taking a bite of the-goo in front of me, I try

to smile, I then let out the fakest of yawns,

roll back over and fall asleep.

The nurse astutely takes my food tray away,

leaving me in my slumber.

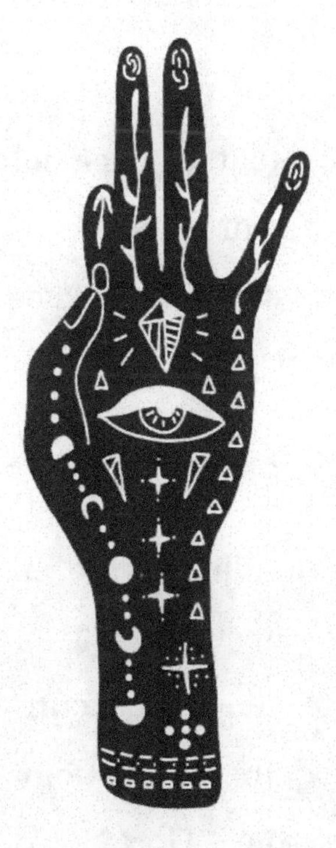

CHAPTER SIX

BURN

I drop immediately back into a transient place where dreams become real, and Patrick and I are forever. I see another door and go to open it.

DOOR 4: THE ELEVENTH BED

Patrick is standing at the end of the hall, looking distant, staring into an empty void. I walk to the end of the corridor, past the reception booth, and he points me towards the vacant room, "Flora, look, this is where you'll find the truth."

I get close enough to ask, what do you mean Patrick? This is just a patients room. The bed is numbered (eleven), they must keep track of inventory.

Patrick's voice slows to a whisper, his lips slightly trembling, "don't you see, this is where the past and present meet."

"What, Patrick, could you be any vaguer?" I ask, waiting for the end of the joke.

Patrick, appearing to not be joking, is now sitting on the edge of the hospital bed, "I'm so glad you finally found me, Flora, I didn't think you'd come.

"I don't understand" (rushing over to his side), "Patrick—what are you talking about?

You left me here. I woke up in the hospital and you were gone!"

I'm shouting, I feel so angry I could ring his neck. If only he didn't look so honest.

He looks at me calmly, "I'm not so sure, and... well, I don't know, but I need you to know I didn't leave you."
"No, that can't be. We had an accident Patrick, don't you remember?"

Patrick, reaching out for my hand, *"don't you?"* He looks at me with sadness on his face, "sometimes, no matter how hard we try, we can't change the outcome—the ending will always be the same."

"What?" I stare at him blankly. What does he

mean by that?

Just as I'm about to have an epiphany—a knock on my door sends me flying into a state of eternal dread. "Flora, it's time for your appointment."

"Ugh—okay, I'm coming. Damn it."

Just a dream Flora, it was just a dream. I pick myself up out of bed and follow the nurse into the depths of despair.

A MILKCRATE MADE OF MEMORY

It was our final appointment. Dr. Powel once again brought out the mysterious milkcrate and placed it before me. "Tell me again, Flora, do you recall anything about this milkcrate at all?"

This time the word falls out my mouth, "Oh my god, that's The Bucket of Lost Dreams..."

"Pardon?" he asks, looking uncertain as to whether I understood the question correctly.

"I named it that. Because of Patrick..."

"Patrick, ok, good. It seems you're starting to piece everything together. Do you remember seeing him the night everything occurred?" he asks, hoping I'll explain what happened and we can all go home.

"DO I REMEMBER seeing Patrick? What a loaded question. "Where is that guy by the way? I haven't seen him since... since..."
I can't get the words out; they seem to be stuck where bubblegum meets eternity. The

thought stretches over my shoe where my memory seems to end."

I sift through each item, laying them out on the desk to examine carefully. Once again, the events appear out of sequence: the taxi, Patrick, Florence, my apartment, beach, ambulance, Gypsy...

Dr. Powell makes a final attempt. He takes Patrick's book out and places it in front of me, I recognize the writing inside the sleeve as my own, *Happy Fucking Birthday, love Flora. Xoxo*

"How about this" he asks.

"It was Patrick's birthday gift, I say."
I turn the page—and the beach suddenly

appears in front of me.

Recalling the events ever so clearly... "I remember I had gotten really drunk the night before, so I went for a walk. The walk turned into somewhat of a bender."

I break for a second to catch my breath and gather my thoughts.

"Patrick and I met there by chance or fate or what-have-you. It was a surprise to us both. He was taking a stroll along the sand and saw me flailing about in the water. I was coming down off a high. Okay, I was dangerously high. Obviously—you know that part of the story, with me being in the hospital and all. He was holding the milkcrate in his hands..." Doctor Powell briefly interrupts, "why would he bring this with him to the beach?"

"Well, there is a good reason. I was pretty pissed at him for walking out on me, so I got really drunk and rounded up all his stuff in the milkcrate. Then I happened to casually drop it off at his friend's place that morning—I guess before the accident happened."

My thoughts turn inward. It all comes flooding back. The weight of the water – with all the drugs I had taken, made it feel like I was walking backwards, when in reality Patrick and I were finally moving forward.

I continue. "For a single moment, we were truly happy, I swear. I remember us holding each other close. I was practically naked for some reason, so he gave me his jacket. Then we called a cab and went home.

Doctor Powell jumps in to clarify, "but you never made it home, did you?"

"I guess not." I say flustered.

This therapy session feels like a lifetime. An hour turns into fifteen seconds. The universe conspires with my past, introducing me to my biggest fear— And that's when, I dare say—I remember what happened to Patrick.

CHAPTER SEVEN
THE REMEMBERING

THE ACCIDENT

My heart sinks to the bottom of my chest, it's all too much to bear. The truth with a capital T had hit me where it hurts. The day is long, as my breath is short. A tear runs down my cheek as I try to recount what happened.

My heart begins to race as my memory sharpens, details I tried to push away reemerge, forcing their way back into my mind. The taxi driver had been driving erratically, swerving between lanes, his speech slurred as he muttered curses under his breath. I had been too drunk to notice, my own mind clouded by alcohol. But Patrick could see what was happening. He had been trying to talk to the driver, trying to get him to slow down. "Hey, man, you need to pull over," Patrick yelled, his voice strained. "Just stop the car. We'll get out here."

But the driver didn't listen. He just laughed; and smirked, in a way that made me shiver, even now as I imagine it.

"Relax and let me drive," the driver snapped, swerving around another car, "I know what I'm doing."

I remember looking at Patrick, the panic in his eyes as he grabbed my hand, squeezing it so hard it hurt. "Flora, we need to get out," he had said, his voice barely above a whisper. "This guy's out of control."

I nodded, too scared to speak, also too drunk to say anything. My heart pounding in my chest. But before I could do anything, before we could even think of a jumping out... a cyclist shot out in front of us, then it felt as though time had stopped.

The deafening screech of brakes. Patrick's scream, as he threw himself over me, trying to shield me with his body.

And then—impact. The sound of metal crumpling, glass shattering, the earth a dizzying nightmare, as the taxi was thrown off course. And then—everything fades to black.

Patrick had been trying to protect us, trying to help. The force of the collision was a blur...the next thing I knew, Patrick was on the ground.

I remember the way his body went limp, as the world around us dissolved. I had screamed for him, reaching out, trying to pull him toward me, but he didn't respond.

Doctor Powell remains silent, as tears stream down my face, and I try to continue. I try to keep going, clutching the milkcrate and cradling it to my chest, while these images fail to escape me.

His expression somber, as he waits for me to finish. He's seen it before, the moment when the truth finally breaks, pummeling through the walls of denial, when the patient's world crumbles to pieces before him.

He'd hoped I might remember gradually—that the truth would come gently, but it seemed to have hit us all at once.

Doctor Powell knew all too well Flora wasn't over-exaggerating. He knew this perfectly well – because he had been there when Patrick and Flora were admitted to the hospital.

THE SECRET HOUR

The thing about secrets is how they are meant to protect those who usually don't want to get caught, the guilty.

It was a secret, Doctor Powell, didn't want anyone to know. The proverbial animal he locked in a cage that he'd never let out—for fear of making things worse.

It was two sides of the same coin. One man's job is another man's nightmare. His job was simply to observe and to listen—and listen he did – a little too well.

The week prior, the operating room on the other side of his office was in use.

They had just brought in a man hanging on for dear life, he could hear them through the air vent. "you've got this, Patrick, come on, stay with me!"

At first it sounded fatal, but then almost by magic or an act of god, his breathing had become stable, and they carried on as usual. Flora had also been taken in at the same time, she was getting her stomach pumped, labeled as high risk in terms of having a probable overdose, whereas Patrick was expected to make a full recovery.

Soon thereafter, life took a turn even Doctor Powell couldn't have seen coming. No amount of fancy doctorate degrees could have prepared him for what would happen next.

On the other side of his office quarters, Doctor Powell could hear the sound of other doctors scrambling to assist.

He had been in the middle of discussing antidepressants with a patient when he heard the machines in the room next door sound, a bunch of beeping in the background, then someone cried out, "quick, he's about to flatline!"

By the time they could do anything at all, it was already too late. They turned off the machines, the room reeked of dead air, and it was done.

The silence was deafening.

He understood when he took this job that this was to be expected, it was a hospital, after all. However, there was something that followed shortly after that he just couldn't shake.

Doctor Powell had received new files on his desk the next morning, he had been assigned a new patient, Flora Blume, who'd made it out of the accident with the patient the hospital just lost the day before. It would be a difficult case as Flora was struggling to remember what happened, and that there may have been cause to believe she was suffering from addiction and mental health issues, leading up to the incident.

He was well aware these types of tragic things happen from time to time – but he was not privy to the type of behavior he saw next, when he overheard the doctors discussing what went on the day before with the patient in question (with Patrick).

"He's an intern; he didn't know the medication would have that effect on him. This is unfortunately how they learn."

"Right, but it's not the first time he's made this kind of mistake!" Her voice reverberating through the airshaft, "I'm seriously starting to think he's doing it on purpose. He needs to be fired."

"We both know that won't happen. Fairview will find a way to make this all magically disappear, and you know it. It kind of makes them look bad if the interns are constantly killing the patients, don't you think? And between you and me, I'd like to keep my job, thank you very much."

Doctor Powell couldn't believe his ears. This couldn't be real—an intern accidentally upped the ante on Patrick's dosage, it was all a mistake? And they were just gonna cover it up?

Easily done, I suppose, they can just say the accident killed him. It was a bold face lie, one which would cost the hospital nothing to sweep under the rug, while costing Patrick his life.

This incident (and I say that with air quotes), intercepted with Doctor's Powell's guilt. He knew he had to do something, anything, but what, he wasn't exactly sure.

When Flora walked into his office that first morning – all he could do was what he was trained to do—he just listened. He softly asked her how she was feeling – then pulled up a seat to hear her talk.

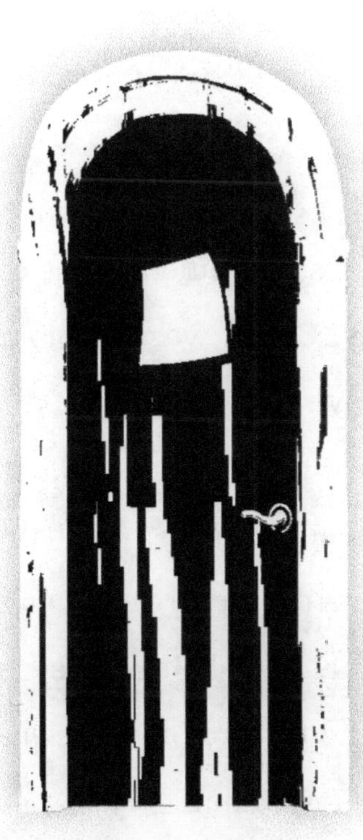

CHAPTER EIGHT

THE FORGETTING

The hospital staff could see the lady coming a mile away, Gypsy was wearing her usual, an overgrown shawl and tacky jewelry, a headpiece with feathers poking out from atop her head, like an old flapper from a nineteen-thirties picture. She was a sight to behold, walking all the way down the hospital aisle towards my designated room. You couldn't miss her,

"Alright, good, She's down that-away!" she hollered, voice billowing off the corridor walls. She stops in the entrance, runs her hand over the door frame, as if to say, I'm here!

She enters and gazes at me staring into the void. "You know, Flora," she states boldly. "Not too long ago, women were called crazy behind these very walls. The ladies, once known as healers—witches—were told they were evil. Then they locked them all up or burned them alive!"

She pauses for inflection. "then along came electric shock therapy and a bunch of pills. Hooray for science!" Her teeth clenching through a fake smile.

"One might say, I don't like hospitals much."

I didn't really hear her; I was busy staring blankly at the wall. The dull ache of loss weighing heavily upon me, leaving me hollow. Adrift in thought, I almost didn't even see her.

The only thing I can do is replay the memory of the accident in my mind. It was the worst of all movies playing over and over again until I naturally combust.

"Flora," Gypsy's voice was soft but firm. I think I recognize the voice, as I turn to see her slowly adjust to the fluorescent lighting.

"Prison is more hospitable than this," she says, trying to get a laugh, her accent unmistakably her own.

Gypsy's presence was like a tsunami that caught me off guard. She walks over to the bed and takes a seat beside me, her expression gentle but filled with remorse. "The hospital called me," she says quietly. "They needed an emergency contact for you and found my card in your purse. I figured, what the hell, I'm not doing anything today..."

I look down at her hands, fidgeting with her nails. I try to place her, I think I recognize her, but just barely.

"Flora, it's me, Gypsy. Do you remember? You came to my home for a reading"

Her face is slightly less blurry than before, she looks presentable, as anyone would after the number of drugs I took wears off.

"Umm, yes. of course, I remember you. Sort of. *Why are you here?"*

"The hospital didn't know who to call, they said you could barely remember your own name."

"Wow, and you actually came? That's really kind." I say, trying to figure out what to do with her.

"Well, honey, when you're as old as I am, an old crone like me– and you meet a gal as drunk as you, that passes out on your sofa, and then finds herself in the hospital the next day – one tends to think she could probably use some help.

Now I feel bad for wanting her to leave. She's funny. "Well, that's probably true. I can use all the help I can get."

"Good guess, I suppose," she winks at me charmingly.

Starting to feel unsure as what to say, "I'm really sorry they called you—I'm a complete stranger—you don't even know me."

"It's okay. Believe it or not, I've been where you are before, and it's the least I can do."

Receptive to her kindness, I'm hoping she's brought me some of that truth serum she cooked up before. A little Jacky D to take me home, sweet mama, take me to the meadows where the green grass grows (a woman can dream).

Instead she just stands there with her face looking droopy. I don't know how to explain I'm just not in the mood for company, "look, thank you and all, I'm just really overwhelmed right now, I can hardly have a normal conversation, I don't even know where to start." My heart shatters into a million pieces before her.

I look at her with my eyes swollen, my face etched with regret, and I can barely contain myself, "he's gone, "my voice barely audible. "Patrick's gone."

For a second, she looks away attempting to think of something to comfort me with, but she can't. "We're talking the same guy, right. Patrick—twin flame—tall, dark, and handsome?"

"Yes, that's him, that's right, you told me he was my twin flame." The thought punches me right in the gut and I want to double over.

"But it's too late now. Even if that were true, which let's face it, it isn't—it's all too late.

He's dead—and it's all my fault." I'm consumed with guilt.

Gypsy, trying her best to help, tries to explain the only thing she truly knows about death. "I hate to break it you, my dear, but you are not that powerful. Nobody gets to take full credit for death's work."

I ignore her hallmark messaging and jump to my next thought. "Wait, I know what we can do... let's find a spell to bring him back! You can help me with that, can't you?"

Gypsy looks stunned.

"I know it sounds absolutely insane, but I'm being dead serious (probably wrong choice of words there)." There is zero detection of sarcasm whatsoever.

Gypsy is completely caught off guard, waiting for this tide to break (my mood), before she tries telling me what she thinks we should do.

My mood instantly shifts from hopeless delusion to sheer rage, questioning Gypsy's ability to see the future at all. "How come you didn't tell me he was gonna die? How could you not have seen that coming? Aren't you supposed to be able to see the future!"

She doesn't even flinch, she's been accused of much worse than being a phony. "Look, honey, I am not the gatekeeper at death's door, okay. It is not my place to evict anyone from this world. Only life itself can do that."

"I think you mean death."

"No, I think I mean what I mean, Flora. It is life that allows us to be here, we just choose the décor," she says wistfully.

"Cute," I say, unimpressed.

Just as I'm about to respond, the nurse enters with some paperwork I need to fill out before my release.

"Perfect timing," I remark, impatiently waiting for this visit to end. She wheels in my cart of food, places the paperwork off to the side, along with a ballpoint pen.

Gypsy decides to wait outside in the hall where I am finally, for once, left unsupervised.

I grab the blank side of the page and start to write.

My Beloved – Letter #2

I am currently holding my breath as I write this. Trying to remember how to release air from my lungs. How can I breathe if you are not here.

I'd be lying if I said I wasn't hurt and saddened by your leaving, but I'd be wrong to say you had any other choice.

Why does air feel so much like dreaming and living so much like a lie. If you can't reach out and touch it – did it ever really exist?

Even still, does the memory of you not matter? Were you not given your own name?

Yet still you come to mind – and every time I meet you there, I get closer to believing in oxygen again. I come that much closer to believing you are still here.

RED TAPE & PAPERWORK

About fifteen minutes go by and Gypsy is acting like she's waiting for me to retire. "Knock, knock!" she says, hugging the door.

The papers haven't even been looked at; I was busy over here trying to convert words into skin. What if Patrick could hear me writing from the other side?

Gypsy, impatient, can see I'm clearly losing the plot and tries to snap me out of this mess. "Look Miss. Flora," she says, we don't have much time. You do not have much time before these people kick you out and start charging rent. So, here's what I think we should do..."

Before I can even ask her what she means, her words are like oil to water. "YOU come home with ME." Abrupt and to the point.

And just like that .... I'm listening.

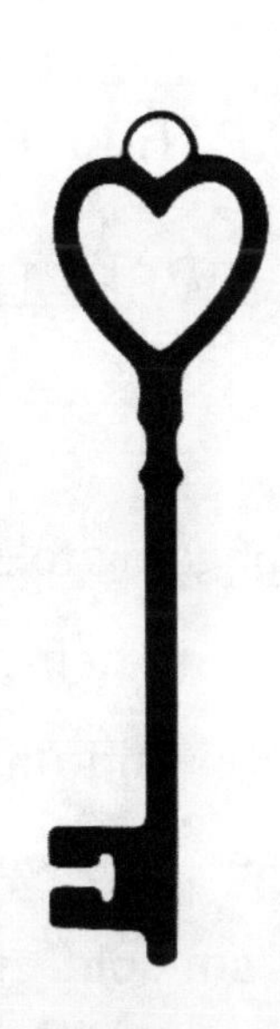

CHAPTER NINE

HOME SWEET HOME

At first, the idea of going to stay with Gypsy sounded worse than being forced to eat hospital food day in and day out. But after mulling it over a sec, she walks me through the details, and I am sold. It makes perfect sense, she believes she was clearly divinely sent to help me, and heck, I won't argue with that—especially since I'm pretty sure I'm late on rent for the third month in a row.

With all that's happened, it seems everyone's greatest concern is surprisingly ME—and my wellbeing. A word so foreign, it was as if I were relearning how to talk.

But as Doctor Powell put it and has said time and time again – along with the many other people put in my care – addiction is better fought alongside those who care. I'm not so sure if anybody truly cares or not, all I know is that a warm cooked meal and not having to worry about paying some bills would take a load off.

They never tell you how heavy it is to carry grief around when coupled with guilt. I feel single handedly responsible for Patrick's death, I feel sick with remorse, with the weight of the world on my shoulders and knowing there's nothing I can do to change it. What's done, is done. There's no going back.

It is beyond me how anyone who goes through the loss of a loved one can just carry on like nothing has happened. How we're expected to just get up and go to work like everything is hunky dory.

From personal experience, the safest place for an addict and drunk to hide from the world's problems is in the back closet, where the secret stash is hidden. If only I could ask Gypsy if she has a liquor cabinet or some secret place she hides her drugs. Yeah, I'm sure that conversation would go over well.

It seems like she'll have me on a pretty tight leash, by the sound of it. The doctors and her, have seemingly conspired to keep me in check, like some militia banning together to fight the war.

I mean, it wouldn't be that far off, trying to save an addict from themselves. It is a lot like going to battle, fighting forces beyond one's control.

I know I'll finally be in good hands, though, but I couldn't help but imagine myself back home in bed drinking it all away. The pain, that is.

Nothing worse than trying to get sober when you are in the worst pain of your life. Just chop my leg off already, it would hurt less.

THE TRUTH

Doctor Powell, standing at my door, looks like he has something important to say. He's holding files in hand and worry on his face. "Flora, Gypsy, can I have a moment of your time?

Gypsy glances at me, and then back at him, "of course, Doc, is everything alright?"

Looking solemn, he begins. "I need to discuss something important regarding Patrick. It's been weighing on me, and I feel it's crucial to be transparent with both of you.

I look up concerned, my expression still, "what's this about?'

He takes a deep breath and explains, "I want you to know I've been involved in an internal review concerning Patrick's passing. After learning about the circumstances surrounding his death, I felt it was necessary to initiate a formal investigation. There seems to have been more to his death than previously thought.

Gypsy, raises an eyebrow, "an investigation? You mean, you're looking into what happened with the accident as some set up?"

"Not exactly. There's actually reason to believe there was a miscalculated dosage administered to him, by either one of the on-call nurses or one of the interns."

The air turns cold as ice. I begin to tremble in disbelief. Gypsy and I cannot believe what we're hearing.

There is never an easy way to respond to the truth when you hear it. The brain is not prepared to do mental gymnastics surrounding facts. My face draws to a close, as I try to process what I'm hearing.

Doctor Powell tries to explain the unthinkable, "I filed a report this morning and have informed Patrick's family. I promise you—we're doing everything in our power to ensure a thorough investigation will be conducted, and the overall handling of Patrick's case will be met with integrity and justice."

Gypsy and I don't move an inch. How could I even begin to comprehend what I just heard.

"Justice!" I scoff. "How can you even use a word like that after what you just said?"

Doctor Powell is at a loss for words. "I am so very, deeply, sorry that you have to find out this way, after everything."

"Oh, me too ... me too, Doctor!" My face says it all. Nothing but complete and utter rage.

Here I've been blaming myself for his death, while this doctor knew the hospital was culpable the entire time. What a total crock.

Upon hearing this, I feel the need to run and hide. I naturally lock myself inside the bathroom of my hospital room, filling a plastic cup up with water to wash away my tears, splashing my face maniacally to feel the cold upon my cheeks.

I need to feel anything, but this. The pain, unbearable, I wait for it to subside.

Bang, Bang, Bang

Gypsy can be heard pounding on the door. "Come out, Flora! It's time for us to go. They're waiting."

I unlock the door and let her in, but I can't let go of the thought of leaving Patrick's body here, after what happened to him. I can't bear leaving his spirit here, leaving this room, leaving him behind.

I clutch onto the toilet bowl and refuse to let go. "I'm not going anywhere!" I scream.

"Don't do this, Flora, I understand you are upset, and you have every right to be, but we have to go now!" Gypsy is doing her very best to persuade me, but I won't budge. She's got me by the legs, tugging at my torso with every fiber of her being, to get me to let go. She grabs me by the hair, and I start flailing. "Flor-a-a-a-a!"

I finally give in, "*okay, okay. I give up already, gosh.*" My hair, now in tangles, my heart ready to jump out of my chest and detonate into thin air.

She gives me a hug, lets me gather my composure, then helps me pack the very few things I have. We take a moment to breathe and then make our way to the front desk to check out.

"Boy, I tell ya, that was by far the worst hotel I've ever stayed at," I say, trying to lighten the mood.

The admin gently smiles, and asks me to sign out, she then hands me over my milkcrate, *Patrick's Milkcrate*, which is now empty.

I can't help but feel that is symbolic, almost as though the milkcrate represented Patrick somehow in his absence.

"You can fill it with new dreams," Doctor Powell whispers, without realizing how incredibly painful it feels to dream at all.

Standing here at the counter, I cannot hear another word. I momentarily slip away, where dreams are always real, and where Patrick can find me.

"It's not your fault, Flora. None of this was," Doctor Powell asserts, trying to find the right thing to say.

But there's nothing to be said. No one can explain away the grief, the loss, the time.

Instead, I simply pick up Patrick's milkcrate and walk away.

Gypsy, smiles softly, a hint of warmth in her eyes. "We start by taking one step at a time," she assures me. "There's no quick fix, but I will be here with you every step of the way."

It was quite a sobering thought. Not subtle whatsoever. Yet, it was exactly what I needed to hear.

I nod slowly, the enormity of what Gypsy was saying beginning to sink in. For the first time in ages, I feel like I'm finally going the right way.

Gypsy suggests taking a taxi home and then remembers that's probably not the best idea. I opt to walk, and she agrees.

"Gypsy?" I ask, "what day is it again?" Not realizing how long I've been couped up.

"November 29th, my dear. Notably, in numerology we add the numbers together. So, two plus nine equals eleven, making today officially 11/11. The time's 11:00 am."

'Why am I not surprised..."

Gypsy smirks, knowingly, like the snow owl glaring over way, seeing everything play out exactly as it should.

The sun is beaming down, uncertainty is upon us. With this milkcrate under one arm and Gypsy on the other, I am relieved to know we are finally homeward bound. *"Thank you,"* I whisper under my breath.

The world is spinning – nothing is the same – but at least I am alive.

Adhuc Coelum volvitur
GLORIA SOLI
PARS
PRIMA

A YULETIDE LETTER

December 25th

Dear Patrick,

I still see you in my dreams. I hear you every time you call out to me.

Maybe you were right, maybe the hands of fate are out of our control.

Nobody knows when they'll take their last breath. We cannot predict the outcome, no matter how hard we try.

You make a different choice, walk through a different door, but the ending could still, very easily turn out the same.

To that end, we may never know. The only thing I know for certain is how much I love you.

– Flora xo

I crumple it up and throw it to the flames

THE END

Thank you to the artists for their contributions: *Fluf, GDJ, Open Clipart Vectors*